GREAT ESCAPES
ACROSS THE MINEFIELDS

BY **PAMELA D. TOLER**

HARPER

An Imprint of HarperCollins*Publishers*

To my husband, Sandy Wilson,
who is the reader in my head and in my heart

Great Escapes #6: Across the Minefields

Copyright © 2021 by the Stonesong Press LLC

All rights reserved. Printed in the United States of America.
No part of this book may be used or reproduced in any manner
whatsoever without written permission except in the case of
brief quotations embodied in critical articles and reviews. For
information address HarperCollins Children's Books, a division of
HarperCollins Publishers, 195 Broadway, New York, NY 10007.
www.harpercollinschildrens.com

ISBN 978-0-06-286069-9 (trade bdg.)
ISBN 978-0-06-286050-7 (pbk.)

Typography by David Curtis and Laura Mock
21 22 23 24 25   PC/LSCH   10 9 8 7 6 5 4 3 2 1

❖

First Edition

EUROPE, 1939-1940

AFRICA, 1940-1942

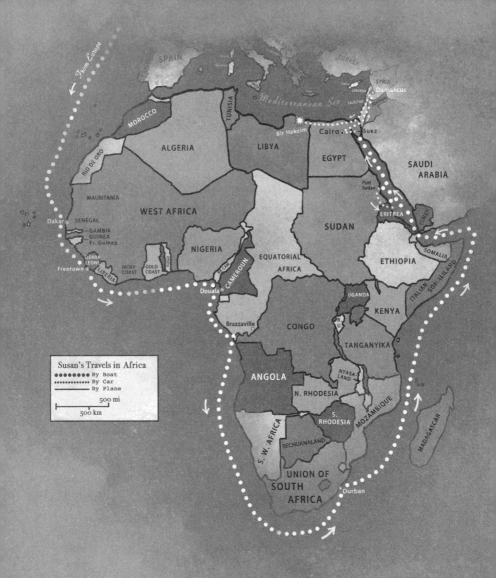

Chapter 1

THE SIEGE

Bir Hakeim, Libya—June 8, 1942

Susan Travers heard the whine of the approaching planes. She put on her helmet and kneeled on the floor of her dugout, waiting for the next German air raid to start.

Imagine you're in a deep underground bunker, she told herself. *Imagine your helmet is a huge metal umbrella that bombs bounce off of, like hailstones from a roof.*

She knew in reality that the helmet would not protect her if a bomb hit, but it was better than nothing. She had lived in a tent at other military camps, but that would have been too dangerous in this Free French outpost in the Libyan Desert. Her home here was a narrow trench dug into the sand. It was ten feet long, four feet wide, and waist deep—big enough to hold a camp bed, a little folding chair with an attached table, and her suitcase. The walls were reinforced with sandbags to keep them from collapsing, and a thin piece of sand-colored canvas stretched over the top to protect her from the sun during the day. But it wouldn't protect her from a bomb any more than her helmet would.

Right now, as she waited for another wave of the German dive-bombers, called Stukas, to attack, she thought it looked more like a shallow grave than a refuge.

Susan could hear the Stukas now, droning in the distance like a vast swarm of bees headed toward Bir Hakeim. They were the worst part of the German attacks, in her opinion. As the sound grew nearer, she felt her heart pound and her legs tremble. It seemed like the bombers' humming was *inside* her head.

Abruptly, the sound changed into high-pitched

screams, followed by silence as the planes dived toward the earth and released their bombs. The silence was almost worse than any of the noises. Five long seconds of quiet as bombs fell toward their targets on the ground.

Susan counted the seconds in her head, the way she had when she was a little girl waiting for the lightning after a clap of thunder. *One, two, three, four, five—*

The shells hit the ground right on time, exploding with a blinding flash. The earth shuddered. Then debris and dust filled the air.

"Please let it be over," she whispered.

Susan knew the siege would have to end soon. General Koenig, the commander of the besieged French forces, had refused to surrender to German commander Erwin Rommel. This meant Rommel would have to come in after them. The French troops couldn't hold out much longer. Susan's garrison was running out of food, water, and ammunition. Soon they would have no choice but to give up.

When the war with Nazi Germany began three

years earlier, Susan had eagerly volunteered to help her beloved France, first as a nurse and then as a driver. But she had never imagined that she would end up in Africa with the First Free French Brigade, fighting to keep the Germans out of Africa.

Susan and the Free French forces under the command of General Marie-Pierre Koenig had arrived at Bir Hakeim on February 14, 1942. After nearly four months in the desert, most of the soldiers wanted nothing more than to leave. But not this way. Not in defeat.

Their job was to help stop the German army from advancing into Egypt. Bir Hakeim was the most remote Allied post, but now, suddenly, their encampment was the focus of Rommel's Afrika Korps. Susan's garrison went from being the least important to one of the most crucial of the war.

The shift happened in late May. Commander Rommel ordered his army to march in a different direction and head straight for Bir Hakeim. For almost two weeks since, the Afrika Korps had rained down artillery shells on the outpost. The

Germans had help as well. They had allied with the Italians, who had sent soldiers, tanks, and other equipment.

Susan and her fellow soldiers were surrounded first by a no-man's-land of barbed wire and anti-tank minefields, and beyond that, the German and Italian forces. Air raids battered the French camp day and night. The fighting stopped only when a sandstorm rolled in from the desert, making it impossible to see either friend or foe.

The French also had another enemy: the desert. Bir Hakeim was an old fort on a sand-blown plateau, a flat area only slightly higher than the land around it. There was no shade, and sometimes, even now in June, the temperature reached as high as 120 degrees Fahrenheit during the day. At night, when the sun went down, the temperature fell below freezing, and the soldiers shivered in their dugouts.

Now, when the dust from the air raid settled, Susan looked out of her dugout to see where the bombs had fallen. The mobile van that served as the general's headquarters was untouched. So was the officers' kitchen, which was only halfway underground.

The general's cook poked his head out of the kitchen tent. He looked up at the sky, listening for the sound of returning Stukas. When it seemed to be all clear, he hurried toward Susan with a small box in his hands.

"For you." He thrust the box at her. "The general asked me to give you some of his special rations. No sense leaving good food for the Germans."

He hurried back to the kitchen, without waiting for Susan to say thank you.

Susan took a quick peek. Canned asparagus and sardines! That would be a nice change from tack biscuits and the canned corned beef the soldiers called "bully beef."

Susan looked at the sky the same way the cook had. She wondered if she still had time before the Stukas came back.

No sign of them yet, she thought.

Susan crawled out of her dugout and ran to the large sloping pit where she kept General Koenig's car. As the general's driver she had her own important job to do: Make sure the car was always ready to go. While gunfire roared on the camp's perimeter, she dug the car out of the sand with her hands, started it, and let it run for a few minutes.

Over the sound of the car engine, Susan heard the Stukas again. "Back already?" she muttered. She shut off the car and ran for her dugout. Once there, she kneeled on the floor again and whispered the Travers family motto as the hum of the Stukas came closer: *Nec temere nec timide.* "Neither afraid nor timid." She'd learned the motto from her father, who had served in World War I, and she had always been determined to live up to it, no matter what. It was thanks to her commitment to the motto that she'd wound up in Africa in the first place. Whenever possible, she had chosen to move toward service in action, even if that meant danger instead of safety.

THE AXIS VS. THE ALLIES

The nations that fought in World War II (1939–1945) were divided into two groups. Germany, Italy, and

Japan formed the Axis powers. All three countries wanted to expand their power. Germany wanted to control all the European countries in which German-speaking people lived. Italy wanted new colonies in Africa. Japan wanted to build an empire in Asia. As the war went on, some people from countries conquered by the Axis powers fought on their side, including Vichy France.

The other side, known as the Allies, was made up of countries that wanted to defend themselves against Axis expansion. At the beginning of the war, Britain, the countries of the British Empire (including India, Canada, and Australia), and France led the war against the Axis powers. As Germany conquered more of Europe, different groups of European refugees—including Poles, Dutch, and the Free French—joined the war on the side of the Allies. China was also an important member of the Allies in the war in Asia. The United States joined the war on the side of the Allies in December 1941.

The Soviet Union signed a treaty with Germany

shortly before the war began. The two countries promised not to attack each other and divided Europe into separate spheres of influence. In June 1941, Hitler broke his treaty promises and launched a massive invasion into Soviet territory. The Soviet Union then joined the Allies.

The United States entered the war on the side of the Allies after the Japanese bombed Pearl Harbor, a US naval base in Hawaii, on December 7, 1941.

Chapter 2

A COUNTRY AT WAR

France, June 1939—Three years earlier

Susan could not believe what Agnes was telling her. Conditions in Vienna must have gotten worse in the fifteen months since the Nazi army marched across the Austrian border. Susan read the letter again.

> *Dear Susan,*
>
> *You know I'd love to see you, but this year it's just too dangerous. Austria isn't the same anymore. The German flag with its swastika hangs everywhere, even in the window of our favorite café. The one that had those delicious pastries, back before*

butter and flour were rationed. These days
we are lucky to get coarse bread to eat with
thin soup.

The Gestapo is in charge here now.
The Nazis do what they please, take what
they please. People are snatched from
their homes and never seen again. Not
only the Jews, but anyone who disagrees
with the Nazis. Even writing this to you
is risky.

Everyone says things will get worse
if Hitler invades Poland. And it is just
a matter of time before he does. We are
thinking about leaving while we still can.

Love,

Agnes

Susan put down the letter and stared out her
hotel window, at the Paris street below. It all
looked so normal. People were hurrying through
the streets on their daily errands as if there were
no threat of war. But her friends were all in agreement—and afraid. They'd written from Germany,

Austria, Czechoslovakia, and Hungary, warning her not to come for her annual visits. They were probably right.

So what do I do? she wondered.

Susan had planned to spend the summer of 1939 the same way she had spent the last few summers: traveling across Europe, visiting friends, and playing in tennis tournaments. It didn't look like that was an option this year, now that Hitler was in power.

I could go back to England, she thought. She could stay with her parents in the country house, where she visited them every year for a few difficult weeks at Christmas.

Not a good choice.

Or better yet, she could stay with Aunt Hilda in London. She always had a good time with Hilda. But Hilda's apartment was small. She couldn't stay there for very long.

Besides, England wasn't really her home anymore, no matter what it said on her passport. She had lived in France on and off since she was twelve, when her parents had moved there for several years. When they went back to England, she stayed. France was the home of her heart.

Susan picked up an unanswered invitation. Gladys Ashe, a wealthy American friend, had invited Susan to spend the summer in her chateau near Poitiers in western France.

There's my answer, Susan thought. Poitiers it would be.

On the surface, life in Poitiers that summer looked like all the other summers Susan had spent in Europe. Gladys threw tennis and hunting parties during the day and extravagant dinners and balls at night. Susan enjoyed them all. But underneath the parties lay the simmering threat of war. It was all anyone talked about.

Susan's friends wrote about the prospect of war with certainty and fear. Gladys and most of her guests knew that war was possible, but they didn't believe it would last more than a few months or that it would affect them directly.

"Honey," Gladys said whenever they discussed

the subject, "I'm staying put. We'll be safe in France."

Susan wasn't so sure.

Then on September 1, 1939, the Nazis invaded Poland. Two days later, France and Britain declared war on Germany.

Over the next few weeks, life in Poitiers changed dramatically. Young men joined the army. Young women volunteered to work with the *Croix Rouge*, the French Red Cross.

Susan knew her carefree summer had come to an end. She wanted to be part of the war effort now. But she didn't want to be a nurse, working in a hospital. She wanted to be on the front lines, where she believed she could make the most difference.

When she thought about it, she had three practical skills that might get her a military job. She was able to shoot a rifle well enough to bring down a bird on the fly—like waltzing, shooting was a basic social skill many privileged young people learned in the 1920s. And, thanks to her father, who taught her to drive the summer she turned seventeen, she was an excellent driver. She could also make basic repairs to a car, like changing the oil and replacing a tire.

Maybe I could drive an ambulance, Susan thought.

But becoming an ambulance driver wasn't as easy as she'd hoped. When she went to the French Red Cross office in Poitiers to volunteer, the woman at the desk told her she would need a nursing certificate first.

"But I'm an experienced driver," Susan argued.

"You have to be trained as a nurse," the woman insisted. "What if you need to give emergency medical help to wounded soldiers? You won't be any good to us, or to them, if all you can do is drive."

"Fine," Susan agreed. "Sign me up."

THE ROLE OF WOMEN IN WORLD WAR II

Women were as important to the war effort in World War II as their male counterparts.

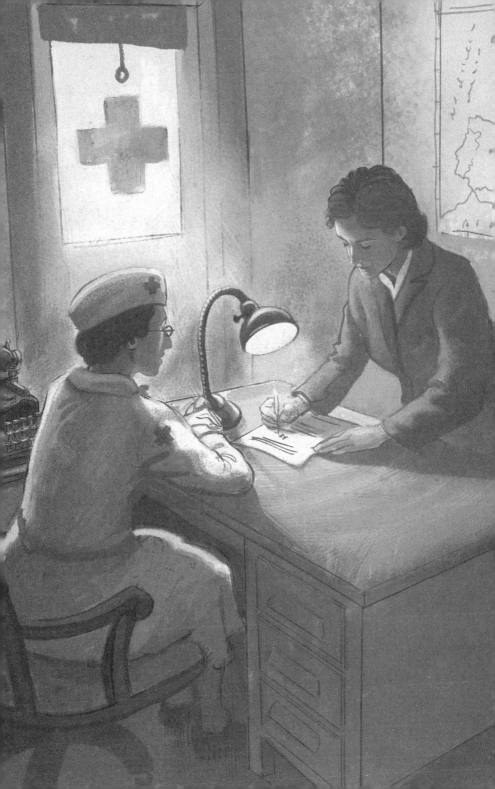

At the start of the war, most women who wanted to volunteer became nurses, either as part of a military nursing corps or through the Red Cross.

But as the war went on, new jobs opened up to women because the armies needed more soldiers. There just weren't enough men to do all the jobs.

In the United States and Great Britain, women joined their own branches of the military. They did not take part in combat, but they did everything else. They worked as radio operators, mechanics, drivers, and air traffic controllers. They helped break enemy codes. One unit of Black American women had the job of sorting through two years' worth of undelivered mail and getting it to the soldiers. It took them three months, but they got the job done. In Great Britain, women helped defend their country as part of antiaircraft units.

In the United States, women who were already pilots served with the Women's Airforce Service Pilots (WASP). They tested new planes and flew them from factories to military airfields. They towed targets behind their planes so airplane gunners could practice shooting at them. Some women taught men to be military pilots. In Britain, women pilots performed similar jobs as part of the civilian Air Transport Auxiliary.

The Soviet Union used as many as one million women in its military, and it was the only country to send women into combat. Some became snipers; others were tank drivers. Soviet women also flew military aircraft, becoming the world's first women to see combat in an airplane.

In countries occupied by Germany, women also served as spies and were an important part of the resistance movement.

Away from the fighting, women worked in factories of all kinds, doing jobs once done only by men. In the United States, the name "Rosie the Riveter" was given to women who helped build planes and other military equipment.

Susan quickly discovered she didn't have a natural talent for nursing. She had little patience for cleaning floors and washing linens, and even less confidence in her ability to take care of people who were ill or injured.

This is not how I can be most helpful to the war effort, she thought more than once during her three-month training period.

Worst of all, she was terrified of giving a patient the wrong medication. Once during a surgical operation, Susan was so afraid to give a patient too much anesthetic that she didn't give him enough. He woke up halfway through the operation, waving his arms in distress!

Susan panicked and jumped back from the machine.

"What are you doing?" the doctor shouted at her. He increased the anesthetic himself until the patient went back under.

"I'm so sorry—" Susan gasped.

"Someone get this girl out of my operating room!" the doctor yelled.

For the rest of the class, the head nurse called Susan "the Public Danger."

But despite all this, to Susan's surprise, she passed the class. With her nursing certificate in hand, she was eager to find the work she wanted—in the middle of the action.

Susan hurried to the French Red Cross office in Poitiers. She had heard the ambulance service was sending a team to Finland to support the small Finnish army, which had been fighting Soviet Russia's much larger Red Army, which at the time was allied with Germany.

When she arrived at the office, she found a line that started at the clerk's desk, went across the room, and ended down the hallway!

Susan took her place at the end of the line behind a grand lady in a fur coat, a chic suit, and a very fancy hat.

She doesn't look like an ambulance driver, Susan thought. Then she saw her own reflection in a window, and she started to laugh. She was wearing an equally fancy suit and an expensive hat that she had bought in Paris that spring.

Finally Susan reached the front of the line. "I'm here to volunteer to go to Finland as an ambulance driver."

"You and everyone else." The Red Cross clerk scowled at her hat.

"I'm qualified." She pulled her nursing certificate out of her purse and pushed it across the desk. "I did the nursing training. And I've been driving since I was seventeen."

The clerk wrote down her name and contact information on the application form. "Don't count on going," he said brusquely. "We've got more people volunteering as drivers than the Finnish army has soldiers."

Susan felt her heart sink. She knew she could be helpful. She just needed a chance to prove it, even if it meant working in the hostile conditions of the Arctic north.

Chapter 3

GETTING TO THE FRONT LINES

Normark, Finland–June 1940

It could be worse, Susan thought as she walked through the makeshift Red Cross hospital. She had helped set up this ward when she and the rest of the French Red Cross team arrived in Finland in early April amid freezing temperatures.

Susan was there as a nurse, not an ambulance driver. Before she could prove her worth, she needed to serve, and being a nurse was the only way she was allowed to help at first. She was taking care of convalescing soldiers, far away from the front, where all the fighting happened, but she was glad to be working.

The young Finnish soldiers in the hospital beds

were grateful for Susan's kindness as well as for the medical care. Many of them had lost fingers and toes to frostbite. Some had been shot or hit by pieces of an exploding artillery shell. Some were ill from exposure and exhaustion. And they were the lucky ones. Twenty-five thousand Finnish soldiers had died in the Winter War against the Soviets, nearly one-fifth of the tiny Finnish army. Some of them had frozen to death when the temperature dropped to 40 degrees below zero. Susan shivered at the thought.

She stopped at each bed as she went through the hospital ward, making sure the soldiers under her care had what they needed before she left the floor. Sometimes in the night, when it was hard to sleep because they were in pain, they needed someone to listen to their stories about fighting the Russians in the freezing cold. Susan could barely imagine the horrible things they had experienced.

Tonight, though, the ward was quiet.

Susan moved a little faster. She didn't want to be late for the news report from London. The Germans had continued to advance across Europe. After Poland, they had marched into the

Netherlands, Belgium, and Luxembourg. Then, one month ago, they had done the unthinkable and invaded France. The newscasters called it *blitzkrieg*—lightning war—because they moved so fast. Susan thought about Gladys and her other friends in France, and she prayed they were okay.

When Susan walked into the kitchen, the other nurses were already huddled around the crackling radio. The BBC's nightly broadcast in French was starting.

"*Ici Londres*. This is London," the broadcaster announced. "Today the German army entered the gates of Paris. People have been fleeing the city since early this morning. No government officials remain at their posts to answer questions from terrified Parisians." The broadcaster paused for a moment. When he spoke again his voice shook. "I have just been informed that the German swastika now flies over the Eiffel Tower."

The kitchen erupted in gasps. One of the other nurses began to sob. Susan felt as if she had been hit in the chest. Her Paris in the hands of the Nazis?

I need to help fight them, she thought. *But how?*

A DIVIDED FRANCE

When Germany invaded France in May 1940, French government officials disagreed about what to do next. In mid-June, French premier Paul Reynaud resigned because he refused to surrender to Hitler. Marshal Philippe Pétain, an eighty-four-year-old World War I hero, became the next premier. He wanted to cooperate with Germany.

Under Pétain's leadership, France signed a peace agreement with Germany. The terms were harsh. Germany took two regions of France that shared a border with Germany: Alsace and Lorraine. Both places had large German-speaking populations. Germany also occupied the northern two-thirds of France, including Paris.

Pétain became the leader of a new French government in the small unoccupied portion of southern France. Its capital was in the town of Vichy. Both Pétain and Germany claimed that Vichy France was a free state, but the cost of its "freedom" was total collaboration with Nazi policies.

While many French people believed Pétain's

decision was the best long-term choice for France, not everyone agreed, especially General Charles de Gaulle. On June 17, de Gaulle escaped from France to Great Britain. The next day, he made a radio broadcast from London. He called on all free Frenchmen to continue the fight against Germany.

De Gaulle was in a difficult position. He was not an official representative of France. In fact, some people considered him to be a traitor. He needed support from other countries if he wanted to build an army to reclaim France.

He got that support on June 27, when British prime minister Winston Churchill recognized de Gaulle as the leader of all free Frenchmen.

With Britain's support, de Gaulle became the leader of the Free French.

Thus France was divided into the Free French (against Germany) and Vichy France (in cooperation with Germany), and both claimed to be the true French government.

Over time, de Gaulle built an army of forty thousand men, a thousand-man air force, and a navy of seventeen fighting ships. He also inspired the growth of a resistance movement in France itself.

It took Susan three weeks to get back to Britain. Once she was underway, the voyage was difficult and dangerous. The ship sailed so far north that it went into the Arctic ice fields and had to alter course to avoid being stuck in the ice. Farther south, they were in constant danger of hitting a minefield or being torpedoed by the Germans. The ship reached Scotland on July 6, and from there, Susan took a train to London.

By the time she arrived in Aunt Hilda's apartment in London several days later, she was tired, hungry, and more determined than ever to do something to help the war effort.

The next morning she set out to find a job that would take her to the front lines, where the armies were actively fighting.

She knew lots of people in London: family members, her father's old army buddies, her mother's society friends, people she had skied and played tennis with in Europe. She talked to all of them, but no one was able to help her. And now she was getting desperate.

"Someone has to need drivers. I'm even willing to work as a nurse," she explained to one of her cousins.

"Why don't you talk to General de Gaulle's people? I hear they're looking for volunteers. Maybe they'll take you."

"Charles de Gaulle and the Free French? That would be perfect!" Susan said.

She had heard the French military commander give an impassioned speech on the radio two days after the Germans marched into Paris. France had lost a battle, not the war, he told his listeners. He called on all free French citizens to continue the fight. Officially, France had fallen to the Nazis. But de Gaulle and his troops, the Free French forces, weren't done fighting.

Susan didn't waste any time. She gave her cousin a quick kiss on the cheek and hurried out the door.

The Free French headquarters in London gave

her hope. It was full of people moving with a sense of purpose. Things were happening here, and Susan wanted to be part of it.

Susan stopped a young woman who was walking by with a stack of documents in her arms. "Where do I go to volunteer?"

The young woman barely paused. "Miss Ford's organizing the nursing service. I'm heading to her office now." She walked away without waiting to see if Susan would follow.

Miss Ford was all business. "We need nurses. If you pass the physical, we can use you. You'll need to provide your own uniform and equipment. Be sure they are suitable for the tropics. Report for duty in Liverpool on August 31."

The tropics? Susan thought. *Where on Earth am I going?*

Six weeks later, the SS *Westernland* pulled away from the Liverpool docks on a moonless night, part of a fleet of almost thirty ships carrying both Free French and British troops. The captain had turned off the ship's lights and ordered a blackout, so it wouldn't be a target for German bombers.

Susan and the other passengers were confined to their quarters belowdecks. She and two other nurses would share a cabin for the trip. Outside, they could hear the sounds of the German air raid over the rumble of the ship's engine. It was the fourth night in a row that German planes had dropped bombs on Liverpool. It was easy to imagine what was happening in the city. Buildings burning. People running in panic. The smell of wood smoke and burning rubber hanging in the air.

Finally, the *Westernland* left the coast behind and entered the open sea. Its destination had not been shared with the ten nurses and fifteen hundred men on board.

"The warrant officer told me some French Foreign Legion soldiers are on one of the ships," Simone said. The Belgian nurse leaned forward as if she had juicy gossip to share. "The Thirteenth Demi-Brigade. Or what's left of them after Dunkirk."

"The Foreign Legion?" Susan beamed at the thought of serving alongside a brigade of legionnaires. They were soldiers from different countries who volunteered to fight for France, and they were some of the most legendary soldiers in the world. Made up almost entirely of men who had left their home countries—many because they were accused of crimes or had other troubles—the Foreign Legion had a reputation for fighting their way out of hostile conditions against almost-impossible odds in wars all over the world. The French Foreign Legion was also an unusual military unit because soldiers swore loyalty not to France but to the legion itself. Susan had been fascinated by the legion ever since she read stories about their adventures overseas when she was a schoolgirl.

The head nurse, May Kelsey, shook her head and laughed. "Makes no difference to me, ladies. Legionnaires might sound impressive, but they bleed like any other soldier, and they aren't any easier to take care of. What *I* want to know is where we're headed. I'm guessing West Africa."

As the ship plowed through the waves, Susan hoped that, wherever they were going, it would be someplace where she could be useful. Where the action was.

THE FRENCH FOREIGN LEGION

The French Foreign Legion is a unique branch of the French army made up of volunteers from many countries.

Men joined the legion because the government of France did not care about their past. Many of them were running away from political, legal, or personal problems. They could change their names when they enlisted, so their histories would not follow them. This is still true today!

For this reason, the other branches of the military and Allied commanders sometimes looked down on the legion. They had a reputation as mercenaries who were only loyal to themselves. However, the legion has historically been key in France's military victories, and one of their mottos is *honneur et fidélité*, honor and fidelity.

France started the legion in 1831 as a way to solve two problems: provide jobs to foreigners who had taken refuge in France and gain soldiers for its war with Algeria. (Algeria ultimately gained independence from France in 1962.)

For forty years, the legion fought in France's colonial wars in Africa and Southeast Asia. During World War II, members of the French Foreign Legion fought for both Vichy France and as part of the Free French.

Today legionnaires come from a hundred and forty countries, including the United States. Many of them don't even speak French when they join. However, after three years of service, they may apply for French citizenship.

Susan Travers remains the only woman to join the Foreign Legion. The French government ordered the legion to accept applications from women in 2000, but to date no other women have been admitted into its ranks.

Chapter 4

LOOKING FOR ACTION

Dakar, French West Africa–September 1940

Days later, the *Westernland* arrived outside the Dakar harbor in West Africa. Susan looked out to see a major port as the ship docked. Dakar was the capital of France's West African colonies and the site of a fortress and naval base. General de Gaulle expected the troops stationed there to join the Free French. Instead, Susan heard the *tat-tat-tat* of gunfire. She quickly realized the Free French had entered into a heated air and naval battle with their own countrymen, the Vichy French.

As days passed on the *Westernland*, Susan experienced the chaos of war for the first time.

Injured soldiers were everywhere, and the sounds of gunfire were constant. Susan helped May Kelsey and the other nurses turn the ship's dining room into an emergency sick bay. When the first group of wounded arrived, Susan quickly discovered this was a different kind of nursing than she had done in Finland. There, she was far from the battlefield. Here, she was surrounded by incoming artillery fire. Susan did her best to focus on the patient lying on the dining table in front of her, but she couldn't block out the battle happening just outside the ship. She kept one eye on the porthole while she worked, watching the water around the ship erupt into geysers whenever a shell landed nearby.

The badly wounded officer lying on the table before her noticed she was nervous. "What's your name?" he asked.

"Susan." She jumped as another shell hit the water.

"Don't be afraid, Susan." He gave her hand a reassuring squeeze. "Their aim isn't very good."

She smiled even though she didn't believe him,

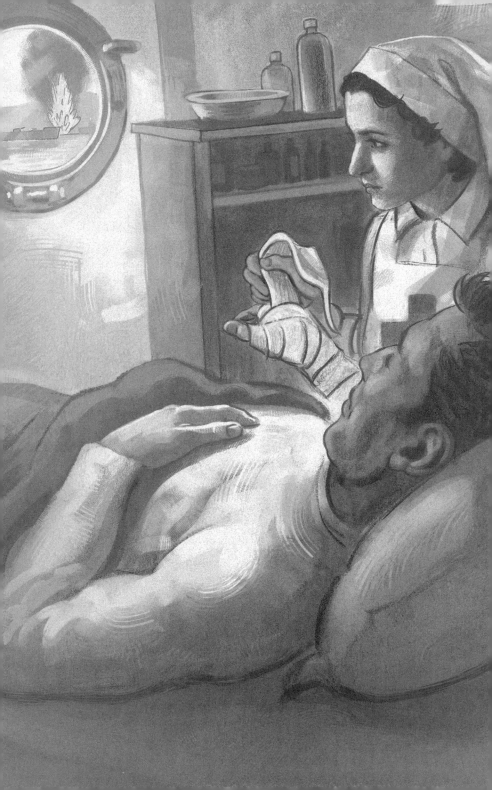

but she appreciated his kindness.

The enemy forces battered their small fleet for three days. Susan and the other nurses watched helplessly as the Free French lost airplanes, ships, submarines, and men. She was afraid, but at last she felt like she was in a place where she was truly needed. She felt more alive than she had ever felt before.

Finally, de Gaulle gave the order to abandon Dakar and retreat to a British naval base nearby in Sierra Leone. The battle was lost.

Susan wanted to go wherever the soldiers were assigned next. Finally, she had found her purpose, and despite the danger, she loved being on the front lines.

In October, news came that the Germans bombed a subway station in London just a few miles from where Aunt Hilda lived. The Germans were killing thousands of civilians with their bombs. And in Vichy France, Pétain signed a law denying Jews the right to work, making it impossible for them to make a living. Susan knew she had to keep fighting alongside the Free French.

But when new orders arrived, Susan and five other nurses were sent to the relatively safe city of Brazzaville, in the French Congo.

While the Free French forces were risking their lives fighting the Vichy French in various parts of Africa, Susan and her fellow nurses were working in a run-down clinic that took care of mothers and babies in the poorest section of Brazzaville. May Kelsey had gotten lucky and got to go with the Free French.

At night, Susan tossed in bed, her body dripping with sweat from the sweltering heat and itching from hundreds of mosquito bites. She thought about Aunt Hilda in London, if she was alive, picking her way through rubble.

It's like Finland all over again, Susan thought. *I'm stuck in the middle of nowhere, useless.* Then her mind turned to her brief time on the *Westernland. I have to do something useful. I have to get back to the front.*

After a few weeks, Susan had had enough. She tracked down General Sisse, the commanding officer in Brazzaville.

"I want to rejoin the Free French forces, wherever they go next," she told the general. "I want to be in the action."

"A cargo ship is carrying supplies to the troops soon," he told her. "I'll sign the papers that will allow you to be on it, if you really want to go."

"Thank you, sir."

"Oh, don't thank me. You're heading straight into danger."

I don't care about being safe, Susan thought. *Millions of people aren't safe in this war. I just want to be useful and do what I signed up for—serve with the Free French.*

A month later, in January, Susan had traveled more than three thousand miles around the southern tip of the African continent to Durban, South Africa. She arrived just in time to meet the Free French soldiers' ship, *Neuralia*, as it pulled into port.

The first person she saw when she came on board was May Kelsey. May greeted her with a big hug. "Travers! Just who I wanted to see."

She dragged her along to the operating room. "You're going to be in here with me, working as my assistant and interpreter."

Susan was glad to see May but not so happy to be in the operating room. She hadn't worked in an operating room since she finished nurses' training, and she was still haunted by that terrible anesthesia incident.

Fortunately, the only patients they treated at sea were a few cases of seasickness. No anesthetic required.

That left Susan with plenty of time to meet—or re-meet—other people on the ship. Most of the members of the French Foreign Legion's Thirteenth Demi-Brigade were on board, back from fighting elsewhere in Africa. Susan had patched up a few of them in the dining room of the SS *Westernland* during the battle at Dakar. She'd discovered that there was more to the legion than the stories that had caught her imagination as a schoolgirl. They seemed like real people now, not simply daring heroes.

One evening she saw an officer she hadn't met

before pacing the decks.

"Who's the tall, handsome guy who wears a green cloak over his uniform?" she asked May later.

"That's Lieutenant Colonel Dimitri Amilakhvari, the new deputy commander of the brigade." May grinned. "Lots of talk about that one. The girls say he's a Russian prince who escaped from the revolution when he was fourteen. But regardless, he is one of the most respected officers in the Foreign Legion."

A few days later, Amilakhvari approached Susan on the deck. "They say if you look long enough at the ocean, its spirit will steal part of your soul," he told her.

"I'm not afraid," Susan quickly replied.

"Fearless? I like that." Amilakhvari smiled. "How are you at playing cards?"

Susan blinked at the sudden change of subject. "Lousy," she told him.

That evening, in the ship's lounge after dinner, Amilakhvari invited Susan to join him and some of the other legionnaires at the bridge table. "Let's see if you're really as bad as you say you are."

Two hands later, he shook his head. "You're right. You're terrible at bridge."

By the time they disembarked in Sudan, many card games later, he and Susan were the best of friends.

Susan and the others camped just outside a small village near Port Sudan. But the village was too small to provide them with any work to do. Susan was so bored she almost wished someone would get sick so she could take care of them!

Amilakhvari just shrugged when she complained. "Boredom," he told her, "is as much a part of war as fear or danger. Believe me, when you're under enemy gunfire for hours on end, a little boredom sounds good."

But everything changed when the rest of the Free French forces arrived, and with them Dr. André Lotte.

Dr. Lotte was the chief medical officer for the Free French brigade. He organized the evacuation of seriously wounded soldiers from the front lines and got them to the nearest first-aid stations for immediate care.

As soon as he arrived in camp, Lotte went straight to the command tent and found the officer in charge of transportation. "I need a driver."

The transport officer threw his hands in the air at one more unreasonable request. "I don't have a driver to spare. All the men have their assignments. You'll have to drive yourself."

"I don't know how to drive. I don't *want* to know how to drive. Do you want men to die because you can't find me a driver?"

Amilakhvari was in the tent, taking care of some brigade business. "What about Susan Travers?" he suggested. "She knows how to drive."

The transport officer was happy to grab at any solution. "Will you accept a woman driver, Dr. Lotte?"

"I'd take a monkey if it could drive."

This is more like it, Susan thought when she got the news. *No more nursing!*

FRENCH COLONIES IN AFRICA

When World War II began, France had fourteen colonies in Africa. Colonies are territories that are governed by other, more powerful countries, often as a result of violent conquest.

Other European countries, including the United Kingdom, Italy, Spain, and Portugal, also controlled colonies in Africa.

Colonies were a source of enormous wealth for the countries that owned them. They supplied Europe with important natural resources, such as rubber, timber, and minerals. Men from the colonies served in European armies, such as the men from France's African colonies who fought for the Free French. Some colonies controlled access to important places, like the Suez Canal or the oil fields in Iraq.

The advantages enjoyed by colonial powers came at a tremendous cost to the colonies themselves. The colonies received little in return for the wealth that was taken from them. The colonial powers destroyed local governments and economies in the countries they conquered. Colonial citizens suffered from systematic discrimination, often enforced by police violence or imprisonment. In the worst colonies, like the Belgian Congo, the colonial power forced its subjects to work on its behalf. The colonial years left a legacy of under-development from which African nations are still struggling to recover.

After World War II, in the 1950s and 1960s, many African countries fought to win their inde-pendence from the European powers. In 2017, the incoming French president acknowledged that colo-nization was a "crime against humanity." In 2020, the president of Algeria announced that Algeria was still waiting on an apology from France.

Chapter 5

FINALLY AT THE BATTLEFRONT

From the Sudan to Eritrea, Africa—Spring 1941

The Free French were scheduled to leave the Sudan for Eritrea at the end of February to help the British defend East Africa against the invading Italian army. Susan and the medical staff would follow them a few days later. They had two days to drive 150 miles.

"We'll never make it in this," she said to the transport officer when she saw the beat-up vehicle the transport division had assigned to Dr. Lotte. It was dented and rusty. It needed new shock absorbers and the brakes were bad. "It's a wreck."

"It's the only one left," he said. "The British kept all the good cars for themselves."

"But it doesn't even have a starter! How am I supposed to start the car?"

"You'll have to start it the old-fashioned way, with the crank at the front." The transport officer made a turning motion in the air, then he gave her an assessing look. "Is that going to be a problem?"

If I say it's a problem, they'll send me back to nursing, Susan thought. *I'm not about to throw away this chance.* She doubted that she'd get another one. "No, sir. Not a problem at all."

Susan woke at four in the morning on the day they were scheduled to leave for Eritrea so she would be ready to leave at six. Since Dr. Lotte was the chief medical officer, their car was at the head of the convoy.

Right where everyone can see me if I have a problem, she worried.

They managed to reach the halfway point on day one without any serious problems. But that didn't mean the driving was easy. Most of the roads were bumpy dirt tracks full of rocks and ruts. The car stalled and stopped working twice.

Both times she had to ask for help starting the engine because the crank was too hard for her to turn. Susan worried that Dr. Lotte would blame her for the problems and ask for a male driver to replace her when they finally reached the Free French camp. After all, an officer's driver was more than a chauffeur. Her job was not just to get Dr. Lotte where he needed to go. She had to be part mechanic and part personal aide. It was her job to keep him safe and to keep him mobile, no matter what it took. Even if it meant driving in combat. And that included keeping this wreck of a car running.

By the time they arrived at their stopping point, eight hours later, Susan's arms ached from trying to keep the heavy car on the narrow, winding roads. All she wanted to do was set up her tent and crawl inside.

The next day the roads were even worse. When they changed from rock to sand, the car got stuck. She had to attach a tow rope to the front so another vehicle could pull it out. And a hundred yards down the road, it was stuck again!

Susan rested her head on the steering wheel for a moment. She was so embarrassed that she wanted to disappear. *No legionnaire would give up*, she told herself. For that matter, neither would a Travers.

"Neither afraid nor timid," she recited her family motto through gritted teeth.

"What's that, my dear?" Dr. Lotte asked from the passenger seat.

"Nothing." She got out of the car and struggled to attach the tow rope for the second time.

"Don't worry," Dr. Lotte reassured her when she got back in the car. "These are not ideal driving conditions. You're doing fine."

"Thank you, Doctor," she mumbled. Susan hoped she would never have to drive through sand again.

They finally reached their destination, a straw-hut village in the middle of nowhere, at seven o'clock that evening. Susan didn't care what it looked like. She could finally stop driving for the day.

Just one more thing to do, she told herself. *Then I can rest.*

She got out of the car and brushed the sand off her clothes. She was so tired she could hardly walk. So tired her teeth hurt. She just wanted to eat and fall into bed, but she needed water for both her canteen and the car radiator. Otherwise it would overheat, and the car would be unusable.

"Where's the well?" she asked the nearest soldier.

He pointed down the road. "Five miles that way."

She groaned, got back in the car, and drove toward the well.

Susan was definitely near the war front now.

While the Free French fought the Italians high in the Eritrean mountains, Susan's job was to drive Dr. Lotte from one field hospital and aid station to another. Week after week, she drove back and forth across rutted desert tracks and up steep mountain roads, following the Free French as they pushed the Italian forces back through Eritrea. When Susan added it up, she realized she had driven more than a thousand miles between the end of February and the middle of April.

Driving the car was hard physical work. The steering wheel was stiff and without electric power steering. She struggled with it even on the few good roads—and most of the roads were awful. More than once she stopped and laid piles of leaves and sticks under the car's tires to get better traction. The parking brake didn't work, so she had to put rocks under the wheels whenever they stopped on a hill so the car wouldn't slide down.

When Susan wasn't driving, she worked to keep the car running. She had learned how to make simple repairs working on the family car with her father. The memory made her smile. Her father had loved that old car. She and her father didn't always get along, but they had spent happy summer afternoons together tinkering with it. He had taught her how to change tires, how to adjust the suspension, and how to check the oil. Now she taught herself how to mend a leaking radiator, replace a fan belt, and repair a punctured tire. When she didn't know how to do something, she figured it out. But there were some things she couldn't repair. Over time, the lights failed and

the brakes stopped working—a scary combination when driving down a steep, winding mountain pass. Some days she wondered how the old heap of a car kept going at all!

By mid-April 1941, Susan and Dr. Lotte were only a few miles away from the front lines of the war.

And she quickly learned just how dangerous it could be when she drove Dr. Lotte to a first aid station three miles from the front lines. The mountain passes were too steep and narrow for the car, so Dr. Lotte and the medical staff rode into the mountains on mules to bring wounded soldiers to the station for care.

Susan parked the car under a bush and looked for a place near the camp to rest for what she knew would be a long wait. She had learned to enjoy a quiet moment whenever she could.

There, that rock in the shade, she thought.

As soon as she sat down, a cook ran out of the mess tent toward her, waving his arms. "No! Don't sit there!" he shouted. "They always shell there."

"Oh!" Susan jumped up. She got a few steps

away from the rock when she heard the whistle of an approaching shell. She froze.

"Run!" the cook shouted. "This way!"

Susan ran. The cook grabbed her arm and pulled her behind a piece of heavy artillery moments before the shell hit. Five more shells hit in quick succession. Each time the impact sprayed them with bits of rock and fragments of the artillery shells. Susan held her breath and ducked her head.

When the shelling was over, she stood up and took a cautious step into the open. She was alive. But the rock she had been sitting on was totally gone. So was the entire mess tent. There were craters in the ground around them.

"Miss," the cook whispered as he tore a piece off a towel that was tied to his waist and handed it her. "You're bleeding."

She looked down. A piece of flying debris had cut her leg open. "Thank you." She tied the rag around her leg to stop the bleeding and went to check on the car. That was her job. No matter what happened.

After that experience, being shelled became a regular event. Susan learned to jump out of her car and scramble for cover at the first sound of enemy airplanes. She pressed herself against any available rock wall or boulder for protection. If there was nothing to shelter her, she flung herself to the ground, with her hands protecting her head.

She didn't know it then, but she was learning skills that would keep her alive during the siege of a desert camp called Bir Hakeim.

Once the Free French got Eritrea under Allied control, their mission was complete, and they moved again. Susan and Dr. Lotte traveled by ship for five days across the Red Sea toward Suez, with the old car stowed in the ship's hold. From Suez, they traveled by land to Cairo, where they joined a convoy of vehicles headed north toward Gaza.

In Gaza, everyone was busy getting ready for the next big push against the enemy. Susan spent her days driving Dr. Lotte between the camp's field hospitals. Soon she and the doctor would follow the Free French soldiers to Syria, where the Germans were trying to win access to the oil fields of the Middle East.

Their final night in Gaza, one of her friends from the Foreign Legion dropped by her tent. "Join us for dinner in the mess hall tonight?"

Susan was thrilled by the invitation. It would be good to be together in one place for an evening before they headed back to the battlefield.

The dinner at the legion mess hall tent was lively. Her friends from the SS *Westernland* were all there. They laughed and ate and drank, teased one another and talked about their wartime adventures.

Halfway through the evening, Amilakhvari stood up and motioned for silence. "We need to give Adjutant Travers a legion nickname!"

It was a great honor. Outsiders didn't get legion nicknames very often.

Susan stood and gave a little curtsy to the room.

"From now on," Amilakhvari continued, "we will call her 'La Miss,' because she is the only mademoiselle among us."

The men roared their approval and banged the tables in applause. They raised their glasses in a toast. "To La Miss!"

Susan beamed. She felt like she was one of the legion now.

AFRICA IN WORLD WAR II

Europe and Asia were the main battlegrounds in World War II, but Africa was also the scene of several important military actions between 1940 and 1943.

When the war began, almost all of Africa was controlled by European nations. The United Kingdom and France had the largest colonial territories, but Belgium controlled a large, rich territory in central Africa called the Belgian Congo, and Italy had conquered much of eastern Africa only a few years before World War II began in 1939.

Both the Allied and Axis powers wanted to control the natural resources and people of Africa, in addition to important transportation routes between Europe and Asia.

The Allied and Axis powers fought over two different colonial issues in Africa. The French colonies in North and West Africa were a source of conflict because their loyalties were divided between the Axis's Vichy France and the Allied Free French. In East Africa, Italy and Germany tried to take British territory in Kenya and Anglo-Egyptian Sudan. If successful, it would have given them control over the critical supply route of the Suez Canal and access to the oilfields of the Middle East.

Chapter 6

A NEW BOSS

Syria–June 1941

The war was still raging. And Susan was right where she wanted to be—in the middle of the action.

Her job in Syria was the same as it had been in Eritrea. She drove Dr. Lotte and the medical staff, including Lotte's new deputy, Dr. Vialard-Goudou, who always seemed to be in a terrible mood, back and forth between their base camp and the battlefields. All the while she heard the constant sounds of gunfire and artillery shelling. Sometimes Susan drove alone to collect wounded soldiers. When she didn't have a passenger, she would give rides to Allied soldiers or local people who were traveling by foot. When she wasn't driving, she scavenged for supplies. Sometimes she traded with local people. Sometimes she dug things out of bombed-out villages. Fresh food to supplement her army rations was always a top priority. In one of her hauls, she hit the jackpot and found a starter and a new battery for the old car.

One day Dr. Lotte told her to stay at the camp while he scouted for a new road that could be used to evacuate the wounded from the battlefield. "Our men say these roads often have land mines planted in them," he told her. "We need to know where the mines are hidden so we don't set them off."

A legion ambulance driver took him away, with a motorcycle following for safety. Once her boss was out of sight, Susan went to the little hut that was her temporary home. She tried to read, but she couldn't concentrate. It was scorching hot. There were flies everywhere. Her mind was on Dr. Lotte.

Later that afternoon, the motorcycle driver roared into camp, shouting, "Somebody, help! We hit a mine twelve miles back. Dr. Lotte's badly injured, and the ambulance driver is dead."

Susan was frantic. She ran to her car without stopping to think.

An officer stopped her. "You won't be any use. Find Dr. Thébault and send him with some troops."

Susan nodded and did what the officer said. When the troops finally brought Dr. Lotte back to camp, he was barely conscious. The mine had almost blown his legs off. It was a miracle he had survived at all.

Susan's nursing skills kicked in, and she helped the medics work on the doctor's shattered leg and foot. As soon as his condition was stable, they loaded him into an ambulance to transport him back to the nearest base hospital for further treatment. Susan knew Dr. Lotte would not be back at work for a long time.

As she watched them drive away, Susan wondered who would take his place.

I should have known, Susan thought when she drove up to the transport office the next morning.

Dr. Lotte's bad-tempered deputy, Jean Vialard-Goudou, was waiting impatiently outside the office.

Dr. Vialard-Goudou was the obvious person to replace Lotte. He had worked alongside Dr. Lotte ever since they arrived in Syria.

I guess he's my new boss. Susan sighed. She had driven him many times before with Dr. Lotte, and she knew he would be hard to work for.

As soon as Dr. Vialard-Goudou saw her, he said, "I demand the transport division assign me a *real* driver. A man."

Susan's mouth dropped open as she walked over to the doctor. "Feel free to check with the transportation office," she told him as calmly as she could manage. He would find out soon enough that no one else was available. Even if someone else were available, she knew her car and territory better than anyone new could learn in weeks.

Vialard-Goudou stormed into the command tent. A moment later he stormed back out and squeezed himself into the passenger seat. "Just drive," he barked at her. "Men are dying while you dawdle."

Susan nodded and got into the driver's seat.

For the next two weeks, Dr. Vialard-Goudou pushed Susan to the edge of her endurance. He put in longer days than Lotte had, which meant Susan worked longer days, too, driving Vialard-Goudou from one field hospital to the next. Instead of letting her rest while she waited for him at each stop, he sent Susan on errands all over the region. She started before dawn and drove all day along the mine-cratered roads. She kept one eye on the road and another on the sky, watching for enemy planes. When she returned to camp late, she couldn't use her headlights for fear of drawing enemy gunfire. Instead, she crept along the dangerous roads in the dark. She was so tired when she finally got back to camp each night that she had to force herself to eat.

Every day, Vialard-Goudou grew angrier and pushed Susan harder, as if he were trying to make her fail. Susan refused to complain, but this seemed to make him even angrier.

It became a battle of wills. In the end it was Vialard-Goudou who snapped. One morning he snatched the keys to the car. "You sit in the passenger seat. *I* will drive."

He turned the key in the ignition, ground the gears, and peeled out of the camp, almost hitting one of the concrete walls designed to defend the camp from enemy tanks.

He is a terrible driver, Susan thought. *He'll kill us both*. She was so tired she didn't care. She fell asleep almost immediately.

She woke with a start when the car jerked to a halt outside the command tent in the main camp.

"Wait here," Vialard-Goudou ordered.

Susan was groggy from the unexpected nap. She opened the car door to get some fresh air and wiped the sweat from her face with the back of her hand.

He's complaining about me to someone. She was certain of it. She closed her eyes, hoping to stop the pounding in her head. Maybe she would get a chance to rest if he fired her.

Vialard-Goudou came back a few moments

later. "Get your things out of the car. From now on, I drive myself."

He jumped into the car without waiting for Susan to respond. She barely had time to grab her suitcase, her tools, and her gun from the trunk before Vialard-Goudou drove away in a cloud of dust.

The old car won't last long with him at the wheel, she thought. But it wasn't her problem anymore.

As she watched Dr. Vialard-Goudou pull out of the camp, someone called out, "Adjutant Travers?"

She turned toward the command tent, still clutching her belongings. *Here it comes,* she thought. *They're sending me back to the nursing corps.*

A tall man stepped out of the tent. The sun caught his blond hair and the embroidered stripes on the epaulettes of his khaki shirt. Susan recognized him instantly: he was the new commander of the Free French brigade, Colonel Marie-Pierre Koenig.

"Yes?" Susan dropped her things to the ground. "Sir."

"You're going to be my new driver." He held out a hand.

Bewildered, Susan wiped her sweaty palms on her shorts and shook his hand. "Nice to meet you, sir." Driving a senior officer was a huge promotion. Only men got those jobs.

She was still trying to understand her good fortune when Koenig asked, "What do people call you? The ones who know you, I mean."

"Those who don't know me very well call me Adjutant Travers, sir. Those who know me better call me La Miss."

"Well, Adjutant Travers, I expect that in the months ahead I'll get to know you very well indeed. La Miss it is."

Chapter 7

ON THE ROAD TO BIR HAKEIM

Bir Hakeim, Libya, Africa—February 1942

Susan waited in General Koenig's office. She was afraid she knew why he had asked her to meet him there.

After months of waiting in Syria to return to the battlefront, the First Free French Brigade had been ordered to go to Libya. They were leaving tomorrow to join the British Eighth Army in the fight for the Western Desert.

No one had told Susan whether or not she would go with them. No one had even talked to her about it. She was sure Koenig was going to leave her behind.

The general walked into his office a few minutes

later. He sat down without greeting her and shuffled the papers on his desk for a moment. His expression was grim.

Here it comes, she thought.

He didn't bother with small talk. "They wanted to assign me a male driver."

Susan balled her fists in her lap. *Of course*, she thought.

"But I told them no. I want you as my driver if you're willing to come." Koenig looked her in the eye for the first time since he came in the room. "It's your choice, La Miss. I'll understand if you want to stay behind. Life in the desert will be hard."

Susan didn't have to stop and think. She'd known what her answer would be ever since she learned the soldiers were going to Libya. "I go wherever the brigade goes."

"Very well." The general pulled a set of papers from his desk drawer, signed them, and handed them to her with a tight smile. "You'd better get to work, La Miss. I believe you have arrangements to make. And so do I."

"Of course. Thank you, sir."

Koenig stood up to leave. Susan was sure his mind was already on the thousand other things he needed to arrange for the brigade's departure. He paused at the door, turned back to Susan, and, to her surprise, saluted her. "Good luck, Adjutant Travers. We will all need it."

The next morning, Susan, General Koenig, and the First Free French Brigade set out for Bir Hakeim, an isolated military camp in the Libyan Desert. Their job was to help the British keep the German commander Rommel and his Afrika Korps from seizing control of the Suez Canal, which was strategically important.

Susan edged the general's car into the convoy headed for Libya. Koenig had been assigned a heavy Ford station wagon when he was promoted to general—a definite upgrade over his previous car, and over the piece of junk that Susan had driven for her previous bosses. Susan thought it looked too nice to be in the improvised collection of assorted military vehicles, rusted-out trucks, ancient cars, and retired buses that made up the convoy. But it was easier to drive a car that didn't break down all the time.

The thirteen-hundred-mile trip from Syria through the Libyan Desert to Bir Hakeim was brutal. The desert sun was bright and relentless. Flies clustered around soldiers' eyes and mouths. Sand filled their food and stuck to their skin.

I would give anything for some hot water and shampoo, Susan thought.

The desert was just as hard on the vehicles. Susan stopped the car as often as she could to check its fuel, oil, and water levels. Each time they stopped, she crawled around the heavy station wagon to make sure the tires hadn't overheated, which could cause them to burst. Everywhere she looked, other drivers were doing the same thing. Making emergency repairs to their vehicles in the desert would be difficult. Maybe even impossible.

Susan and the Free French soldiers finally reached Bir Hakeim on February 14, 1942.

British soldiers hurried over to greet them.

They had been stationed at the isolated position for several weeks and were eager to turn it over to the French.

Susan looked around in disbelief. Someone had told her that *bir* meant "water" in Arabic. She had expected the post to be built around an oasis. But instead of palm trees, there were patches of dry, thorny scrub scattered on a flat plateau of sand and stone. The stark desert stretched toward the horizon in all directions with no water to be seen. The remains of an old stone fort stood at the southwest edge of the camp. Farther away, to the west, she made out two other shapes.

Susan pointed at them. "What are those?" she asked a British officer.

"They used to be tanks to hold water," he said, "But they're broken now. Empty. Just covered with sand."

She looked around again. "Is this all there is?"

He nodded. "Welcome to the end of the line."

Chapter 8

A DREADFUL OVEN OF A PLACE

Bir Hakeim, Libya, Africa–February 1942

Susan looked around the empty plateau at Bir Hakeim. She had no way of knowing that in a few months, she and the rest of the Free French would be surrounded by the Germans and under siege. Right now the only thing she was worried about was where she would sleep.

Probably in the car again, she thought with a sigh. There wasn't any place where it would be safe to pitch her small canvas tent.

"Adjutant Travers." Someone tapped her on the arm. She turned to find one of the legion's engineers. "Colonel Amilakhvari had us build a dugout for you. Could you come inspect it?"

"Of course," she replied, following him to a spot only a few yards from the van that served as General Koenig's mobile headquarters. A group of young soldiers waited next to a long, narrow hole in the ground. Its walls were lined with sandbags and a canvas top that could be rolled across it as a roof.

"To protect you from the sun and the cold," one of the legionnaires explained. He pulled the material over the hole and connected it to the other poles, showing her how it worked.

The engineer who had led her to the dugout helped her step down into her new home as if he were escorting her to a ball. The men stood around its edge, waiting to see if she approved. She gave them the courtesy of inspecting it thoroughly.

It was small. It was different than anywhere she'd slept before.

But it's definitely better than sleeping in the car, she thought.

She looked up at the watching engineers, sank into the most elaborate curtsy that she could manage in a pair of khaki shorts, and flashed them her best smile. "Welcome to Chateau Travers!" she said with a flourish.

Laughing, they bowed in return.

Maybe they could help me solve my next problem, too, she thought.

"Any idea where I can keep the general's car?" she asked.

"Next time ask us for something hard," one of them said. "We have holes in the ground for everything. Come this way."

"The British built an underground maze of dugouts," the engineer explained as they walked. "Small ones for people to sleep in and larger ones for the messes and meeting spaces." He stopped and gestured at several large sloping pits. "These are garages. Since you're the general's driver, you get first pick."

Susan chose the "garage" closest to her dugout and carefully nosed the station wagon down into the hole. Borrowing an idea from her new sleeping quarters, she packed the walls nearest the engine with sandbags. She covered the rear of the car with a piece of camouflage material.

There, Susan thought. The car was as protected as possible, and close enough that she could check on it every day. She brushed her hands together. *I guess my work is done.*

Everyone else had plenty to do.

As soon as they arrived, the men of the Free French brigade improved the system the British had created. Susan watched as they dug more slit trenches, both for sleeping and for defense purposes, as well as larger dugouts for command posts.

Looks like I'm not going to be the only person sleeping in a hole, she thought.

When they finished expanding their living quarters, the brigade set to work improving Bir Hakeim's defenses. The post was already protected by a square mile of barbed wire, trenches, and explosive land mines buried in the sand. The French added thousands more mines and set up anti-tank and anti-artillery guns. If Rommel decided to attack Bir Hakeim, they would be ready.

There was little Susan could do to help while the rest of the brigade prepared and waited for an attack that might not come. But she had her own responsibilities. She checked on the general's car each day. Several times she drove him out of Bir Hakeim with a small group of soldiers. Each time, they spent two or three days in the desert, mapping the area and looking for signs of the enemy. She loved those trips.

But for the most part she was bored and lonely, two conditions that made the discomforts of the desert harder to bear. Bir Hakeim was a dreadful oven of a place. In the day, it was so hot the haze that rose from the sands made her eyes burn and her head ache. So hot the sweat evaporated immediately from her skin, leaving an itchy crust of salt behind. The only relief came from an occasional light breeze, which brought torments of its own by whipping the sand into funnels.

At night, the temperature dropped to below freezing. Susan shivered in her cot, covered by every piece of clothing she owned. Sometimes a sandstorm would roll in from the deep desert. They would hear a rumble in the distance. Then a dark cloud of wind and whirling dust would rush through the camp, leaving injured men and damaged equipment behind.

It was almost a relief when they got the news that Rommel and the Germans and Italians were headed straight to Bir Hakeim. Finally, something was happening.

The first enemy tanks appeared at Bir Hakeim on a moonlit night at the end of May 1942. Susan watched dozens of Italian military tanks roll into view, firing as they came. Behind them, trucks carried soldiers and towed artillery pieces.

All around her, soldiers moved into action to defend the base.

And then enemy shells began to fall. Susan grabbed her helmet and sought safety in her dugout. She could no longer see the fighting, but she could certainly hear it. Land mines exploded, lighting up the sky as they destroyed the enemy tanks that rolled over them. The French artillery guns shot at tanks that got past the mines.

Shortly before the main attack began, Colonel Amilakhvari poked his head into Susan's dugout.

Susan scrambled to her feet. "Sir?"

"I don't think you'll need this," he said, handing Susan his rifle, "but it might make you feel better to have it. Just in case."

She nodded. "Thank you, sir," she replied, taking the firearm with trepidation. He was right. And she held it on her lap for the rest of the night as bombs fell around her.

The next morning, Susan heard a bugle call all-clear. The fighting had stopped—for now. She slowly climbed out of her dugout, blinking at the harsh sunlight.

When she spotted Colonel Pierre Masson, General Koenig's top aide, walking away from headquarters, she hurried over to him.

"How bad was it?" she asked.

A grin split his dirt-stained face. "For us, La Miss, it was not bad at all. We only lost one big gun. But for the Italians—very bad. We destroyed thirty-five of their tanks."

The news made Susan smile, too. "Well, that's good."

"Yes. But it's just one battle," Masson said as he walked away. "They'll be back."

Susan knew Masson was right.

Over the next few days, the German army arrived to support its Italian allies. A stream of tanks and trucks full of German soldiers circled Bir Hakeim. When they got too close, French guns fired at the enemy vehicles. Colonel Amilakhvari and some of his men conducted hit-and-run attacks on the German convoys. But the Germans kept coming. Soon Germany's entire Afrika Korps surrounded Bir Hakeim: over forty thousand men and hundreds of tanks.

One night General Koenig came to Susan's dugout. "I'm expecting a convoy tomorrow to transport the wounded out of the battle zone," he said. "You should go with it. The fighting will only get worse. More dangerous."

"No, sir." Susan shook her head. "If the brigade stays, I stay."

The general stared at her for a moment. "Very well, then."

It turned out to be a lucky choice. The Germans attacked the convoy on its way to headquarters. All the wounded soldiers were captured or killed.

Had Susan been with them, the same would have happened to her.

The next night an Allied supply convoy managed to sneak past the Germans under cover of darkness. It carried food, ammunition, and an order from the Eighth Army high command to the commanders of all six posts on the line.

Soon after the convoy arrived, General Koenig called her to his headquarters.

"I just received orders from headquarters. All female personnel are to be sent away from the battlefront immediately."

"That means the nurses," Susan objected.

"That means the nurses *and you*," Koenig said.

"But—"

"There's no point in arguing. Your name is on the list."

Susan took a deep breath and counted to ten to try to calm herself. "Can I come back when the danger's over?"

"Hmm." Koenig hesitated. His eyes flickered for a moment, the way they did when he was thinking his way through a problem. Then he gave Susan a sly smile. "The workshop at headquarters back in Tobruk has a new staff car for Colonel Masson. No one has had time to deliver it here. I don't think the British could object to you delivering an important liaison vehicle, once it's safe to return."

Susan grinned.

Koenig waved her off. "Be ready to leave in the morning."

Safely at headquarters, Susan went to see if Colonel Masson's car was ready for delivery. She wanted to head back to Bir Hakeim as soon as possible.

The car was ready, but the news from Bir Hakeim was bad. "The post is surrounded by the Germans and Italians," the mechanic said. "There isn't much hope for them now."

Susan's chest ached at the thought that her friends—her family, really—were facing danger without her. She *needed* to get back to them.

With the excuse of delivering Colonel Masson's car, she arranged to join a convoy that was leaving the next morning for the post nearest to Bir Hakeim.

But once she arrived, the commander at that post refused to let her go farther. "You'd be driving to your death. It's all but over at Bir Hakeim. They are surrounded."

Susan's throat tightened as she wondered whether the friends she had left behind in Bir Hakeim—Koenig, Masson, Amilakhvari, and the rest—would even be alive to welcome her back.

She reluctantly stayed at the post for three days, sleeping in her car and making herself useful as an extra driver. On the third day, good news came. The French had pushed back the enemy. The Germans were retreating—for now.

A supply convoy was heading to Bir Hakeim that night. Susan wrote a note for them to deliver to General Koenig: *I am at B Echelon with Masson's car. Permission to return? Adjutant Travers.*

The answer came back the next day. *Permission granted. Koenig.*

Chapter 9

OUTNUMBERED TEN TO ONE

Bir Hakeim, Libya, Africa—June 1942

Susan set off across the desert toward Bir Hakeim almost alone. Most of the other traffic was going in the opposite direction.

It looks like they're running away, she thought. *The Germans must be on the move again.* She sped up, hurrying toward Bir Hakeim as if she were in a race with Rommel.

In fact, Rommel's retreat *had* been short-lived. Bir Hakeim would soon be surrounded again. This time there would be no reprieve.

When she arrived, General Koenig welcomed her back with regret. "I can't order you to leave again," he said. "There's no way for you to get out now."

The battle resumed on June 1, the day after Susan returned. Stuka dive-bombers made their screaming descent five times that afternoon. The French antiaircraft guns replied with their rapid *ack-ack-ack*.

In between the raids, Susan ran to the pit where she had left the general's car. She wasn't sure if it would still run after several days of standing idle while she was gone. She dug it out of the sand with her hands. Then she got in, crossed her fingers for luck, and turned the key. The Ford's engine ground once, twice, then started.

Whew! Susan let out a breath. She wasn't sure what she would have done if the car hadn't started. She patted the steering wheel. "Good girl. I'll be back every day from now on."

The next day, Susan watched from her dugout as an enemy vehicle approached the camp. Two Italian soldiers raised a white flag—that meant they came to talk peacefully to General Koenig.

From afar, it looked like the conversation was short. The Italians had brought a message from General Rommel. Bir Hakeim was completely

surrounded. If the Free French did not surrender immediately, Rommel would continue the attack and kill them all.

"I am a member of the French Foreign Legion. We do not surrender," Koenig answered. "As long as we still have our weapons, we will fight."

The day after that, Rommel once again demanded their surrender. This time two British soldiers who had been captured by the Germans delivered the message. They crawled into Bir Hakeim on their stomachs and gave Koenig a handwritten note from General Rommel: *Further resistance will only lead to more deaths. You will suffer the same fate as the two British brigades we destroyed the day before yesterday. We will stop firing as soon as you show the white flag and come out without your weapons.*

Koenig responded by firing the big artillery guns at the enemy camp.

On June 5, Rommel made a final attempt to offer Koenig surrender terms. Three German officers drove up to a legion position early in the morning and demanded to speak to the general.

He refused to talk to them and gave them five minutes to get out before he turned his guns on them, white flag or no white flag.

And so the battle raged on. For Susan, the days settled into a pattern. She started each day by digging out the general's car from the sand that constantly blew over it. With her one job done, she hurried back to her dugout to sit out the day's attacks.

Each day she shuddered at the all-too-familiar sounds of the Stukas' sirens as they dove down on Bir Hakeim and the firing of German artillery. Between the planes' bombs and the artillery shells, clouds of sand filled the air, making it hard to breathe.

On one particularly bad day, Susan felt as if the enemy shells were seeking *her* out, specifically. One shell exploded just a few feet away from where she sat in her dugout. Two more followed it.

"I'm not a military target!" she yelled at the German gunners in the distance.

Somehow, the French held off the Germans, even though they were outnumbered ten to one. Small raiding parties went out every day to steal German supplies. They brought back fuel, water, and vehicles—just enough to keep the camp going.

By June 9, Susan wondered how much longer the French could survive at Bir Hakeim. Despite their raids on the German forces, they were running out of food, water, and artillery shells.

Would she make it out of here alive? Would any of them?

That evening, Susan saw a group of senior officers go into Koenig's headquarters.

She sat on the floor of her dugout and waited for someone to bring her the news. She knew it would be bad. She leaned her head against the sandbags that lined the walls and tried to forget how hot and afraid and miserable she was.

She pictured taking a warm bath with lots of bubbles, putting on the lilac satin dress that had been one of her favorites, and walking into an elegant Parisian restaurant to have dinner with Gladys and her other friends from the happy days before the war. She would order smoked salmon, a perfectly cooked steak, a mound of fried potatoes, and a bowl of vanilla ice cream.

Her stomach growled as she imagined the ice cream sliding down her throat. She opened her eyes and looked in her provisions box. She knew there was nothing in it worth eating. She had four bug-infested biscuits. There was only a few inches of gritty water left in her canteen. Just like the last time she looked. She sank back against the wall and closed her eyes again.

She was almost asleep when she heard the sound of boots on gravel near her dugout. She rolled back the canvas cover and saw General Koenig standing in the darkness. "Sir!" She jumped to her feet and smoothed out her khaki shirt as best she could.

"We can't hold out much longer, La Miss," he said. "The high command has given us permission to pull out. We're going to break through the enemy's lines tomorrow night. We're taking everyone and everything with us. The legion leaves no one behind." He turned to leave. "You've got twenty-eight hours to prepare."

All through the day of June 10, while the fighting continued around them, Susan and the troops at Bir Hakeim prepared for their escape.

Susan's main job was to be sure the general's car was in good shape for the dangerous drive across the desert. As she did every day, she checked the tires, the gas, the water, and the oil. Then she checked them again. There was no room for mistakes. She lined the car with sandbags, to protect herself and her passengers from bullets and mines. She put Koenig's papers and machine gun in the back.

She had just finished packing her own things and was putting them in the car when one of the general's aides walked up with a hammer. Without saying anything, he broke the glass out of the windshield.

"What are you doing?" Susan demanded.

"We have orders to smash all the windshields. If an enemy bullet hits the glass, it will crack and you won't be able to see out."

If a bullet hits the windshield, Susan thought, *I'll probably be dead.*

Chapter 10

AN APPOINTMENT WITH HONOR

Bir Hakeim, Libya, Africa–June 1942

It was almost midnight, the hour when Susan and the other drivers would break through the German lines, following a safe path the engineers had cleared through the minefields around the camp.

As midnight approached, the brigade finished the preparations for their escape. Men loaded weapons and wounded soldiers into the vehicles that were still running. They destroyed anything they couldn't take with them, so the enemy couldn't use it. Nothing and no one would be left behind for the Germans.

The officers used some of their last precious water to shave and changed into clean uniforms.

Susan realized they wanted to look like the proud soldiers they were as they risked their lives for what could be the last time.

She decided to follow their example. She drained the last bit of water from her canteen and used it to wash her hands and face. She adjusted her uniform beret at a jaunty angle. "For courage," she told herself. *"Nec temere nec timide."* Neither afraid nor timid.

While the convoy formed, Susan watched Colonel Amilakhvari walk down the line of men and machines, reminding each group of men of their instructions. "Stay in a straight line! Don't stop for any reason, and be as quiet as possible."

Susan's stomach twisted with nerves as she went over the car one last time. She had started the engine every day, but she hadn't driven the car for several weeks. The Ford had stalled several times back when they had gone on scouting trips in the desert and had been hard to restart. If it stalled tonight, it could be deadly. She turned the key, and the engine roared to life.

"Please don't let me down," she whispered.

She inched the car into position behind the three battalions of foot soldiers who would lead the escape. The spot where the Free French would meet the British forces was twelve miles south of Bir Hakeim. Susan knew they would be the most dangerous miles she had ever driven.

General Koenig came out of his headquarters right on schedule. Like his officers, he was freshly shaven and dressed in a crisp uniform. He looked every inch a commander.

He paused for a moment and looked at the thousands of men who waited silently under a moonless sky for his command. Susan knew they were eager to follow him in this bold attempt. No one wanted to surrender after having fought so hard against the Germans.

Koenig raised one hand and nodded at his troops.

Then he stepped into the back seat of the car. "While you drive," he told Susan, "I'm going to stand on the back seat and watch through the observation hatch on the roof. Understand?"

Susan nodded.

Koenig looked at her more closely and frowned. "And put your helmet on!"

Susan pulled off her beret. She jammed on the tin helmet, making sure it was secure.

The signal came for the convoy to move. The first armored machine-gun carrier moved forward with the foot soldiers, ready to fire if the Germans discovered the French were escaping. Susan put her car in gear and drove toward the minefield. Behind her, the line moved slowly in single file.

She had only gone a short distance when an explosion in front of the car made Susan jump in her seat.

"What was that?" she asked the general.

"The first machine-gun carrier went off the path and hit a mine."

Two more explosions followed as more of the light armored vehicles strayed into the minefield.

With horror, Susan realized that she had gone off the path as well. She could hit a mine at any moment.

Silence and surprise had been the keys to General Koenig's plan. He'd counted on the Germans and Italians sleeping while the Free French slipped away.

Now the enemy was awake and ready to fight. Red and green flares lit up the sky. The sound of enemy machine guns shattered the silence.

This is it, Susan thought. *This is the end.*

Enemy shells exploded around the Ford, showering it with bits of hot metal. Ahead of her, a Bren carrier drove into a German machine gun nest and knocked it out of action. Legionnaires on foot rushed at the enemy's big guns.

"They're risking their lives so we can make it out," Susan realized. She was awed at their bravery.

"Turn the car around," General Koenig ordered.

"Yes, sir." Susan turned, and the other vehicles followed.

Behind her, the general directed her through the minefield, back to the path the engineers had cleared. "Turn to the right and go around that car. Quickly! *Quickly!*"

While she turned, he shouted instructions to his men, directing them to fire at the Italians and Germans. "Fix your bayonets and keep moving forward. Don't hesitate. Quickly!" he repeated.

Suddenly, there was a flash and a loud *boom*. The car ahead of them, where Colonel Amilakhvari was, flew into the air.

"No! They hit a mine!" Susan screamed and stomped on the brake. She could hit one too if she wasn't careful.

Moments later, Colonel Amilakhvari emerged from a cloud of black smoke. He stood outlined against the burning vehicle, a grenade in one hand and a gun in the other. Unshaken, he strode toward a group of foot soldiers who had sought protection from the German guns behind a truck.

"What are you doing?" Amilakhvari bellowed at them. "Fix your bayonets! Attack the enemy! Are you cowards or are you legionnaires?"

The men did as they were told.

Koenig waved Amilakhvari to his car. The colonel jumped in the front seat next to Susan.

"You're not hurt!" Susan said in amazement.

Before he could answer, Koenig barked, "What are you waiting for? Drive! Straight ahead as fast as you can go."

Amilakhvari grinned at Susan. "Drive!" he repeated.

"Yes, sir!" Susan quickly steered around the burning wreckage of Colonel Amilakhvari's car.

"Get to the head of the convoy," Koenig demanded. "The rest will follow us."

Susan pulled past the other vehicles to take the lead.

Driving as fast as she could through the dark, Susan felt finally free, powerful, sharp. She had sat in her dugout for too long, watching the Free

French do their jobs so well. Now she had the chance to do hers.

This is why I volunteered in the first place, she thought.

All her senses seemed more precise. She saw every firework made by German artillery in the sky. She heard the whine of the car's engine as she pushed it to go even faster through the darkness. She felt power vibrate up through the cool metal steering wheel.

"Watch out for that hole!" The general gestured with his pistol. "And that one!"

So that's *what they mean by a "back-seat driver,"* Susan thought. A bubble of laughter rose in her throat. She tried to swallow it down, afraid it would turn into hysteria.

There was no point in reminding the general that each German shell created a new hole when it landed. She couldn't avoid them all.

More explosions lit up the sky. Susan passed vehicles destroyed by mines or enemy shelling. She hoped desperately that her car would not become one of them. German bullets flew around them, and she drove faster. Other vehicles followed their lead.

At one point something heavy slammed into the back of the Ford.

"Have we been hit?" she asked Amilakhvari, who was watching the road behind them.

"Not by the Germans," he said. "One of our own cars ran into us."

A few minutes later, Koenig snapped at Amilakhvari, "Stop firing your gun. It makes it easier for the Germans to spot us."

"I'm not firing my gun," Amilakhvari answered.

"Then what's all that noise I hear?" Koenig demanded.

"It's the Germans shooting at us!"

With bullets raining down around her, Susan drove on until she and several of the other cars drove out of the enemy's defensive line.

"We made it!" Susan cheered.

"That's the first one," Koenig said.

"First one?" Susan asked. "What do you mean, first one?"

"The first line of German guns."

"There are more?" Susan's voice quivered slightly.

"Two more," Koenig said. "Just keep driving."

Susan felt as if she had been driving for hours. They had lost the other vehicles. She had no idea how far they were from the spot where they were supposed to meet the British. She kept thinking they had to be close—they couldn't go on like this—but she couldn't see anything.

At least the firing had stopped.

Amilakhvari pulled out his compass. "We need to head south."

Susan stopped the car so he could take a better compass reading. With the car still running, she relaxed for the first time in four hours. Her hands were stiff from holding the steering wheel so tightly for so long. Her neck and shoulder muscles ached. She was desperate for sleep, but she knew that she would have to continue on.

Amilakhvari got out of the car. He hesitated.

General Koenig poked his head through the roof. "What are you—"

Amilakhvari put his hand over the general's

mouth. "Shhh," he hissed.

A second later, Susan heard it, too—men speaking German nearby.

Someone called out, "Halt! *Wer ist da?*"

Susan understood—a German soldier was asking who was there.

Amilakhvari jumped back in the car. "Drive!" he yelled.

Susan stomped on the gas pedal.

Bullets hit the outside of the car. Susan heard shouting and the roar of an engine behind them. She snuck a glance behind her and saw that several German armored cars were now chasing them.

"Come on," she muttered, begging the car to go faster, and terrified of what would happen if she pushed it too hard.

She zigged and zagged across the desert, trying to lose the Germans who were tailing them.

"There!" Koenig pointed to a place where the land dipped behind a small dune. She pulled into it.

The armored cars sped by. Susan waited to see if they turned back. She sat still, her hands trembling on the wheel, trying to breathe.

"You've lost them," Koenig finally said. "Keep going."

Susan turned around and drove back out into the open desert. There were no more Germans in sight.

When the first light of dawn streaked the sky, Koenig told her to stop.

"I'll drive now," he said. "Maybe the ride will be a little smoother."

Be my guest, Susan thought. She could use the rest.

Koenig sped off.

Susan smiled to herself when she noticed that he wasn't any better than she was at avoiding the holes caused by shells.

Not so easy after all, is it, she thought.

She stretched out in the back seat. As she drifted on the edge of sleep, she realized she'd misunderstood Koenig's desire to take the wheel.

"All of my men are dead," Koenig said in a low voice. "I should never have tried to escape like this."

"You had no choice," Amilakhvari told him. "You did the right thing."

"No." Anger at himself filled every word. "I failed my mission. I failed my men. I will stop if I see a German vehicle. I want to surrender."

"General Koenig!" Susan bolted upright in the back seat. She couldn't believe what she was hearing. "How can you think about giving up? Stop feeling sorry for yourself. And if you can't do that, think about us. I can't speak for the colonel, but I know I don't want to become a prisoner of war with you. The French Foreign Legion does not surrender, remember?"

Koenig was silent for a moment. Then he nodded. "You are right," he said. "We must go on."

Susan surprised herself with her outburst. She knew it was no way to talk to her commanding officer. But he'd needed to hear it. And he'd listened.

Whatever happened after this, Susan would always know that she had the general's respect. She had earned his respect by speaking the truth.

"Let me drive again," Susan said.

Koenig stopped the car and let Susan take the wheel.

As they traveled through the morning light, Susan and the officers drove past the burned remains of British vehicles, abandoned in the desert after an earlier battle. They stopped at a small cemetery, where soldiers from New Zealand were buried, and saluted the fallen.

"They traveled a long way to die in this awful place," Amilakhvari said.

The three were silent for a moment. They knew they also might die in the Libyan Desert. But there was nothing to do but keep moving forward.

Hours later, Susan at last spotted something in the distance. "Do you see that up ahead?"

Amilakhvari squinted to see what she was pointing at. "It looks like trucks."

"German trucks?" Koenig asked.

The colonel looked again. "No! Those are British trucks. We're in Allied territory. We made it, La Miss!"

Susan slumped back against the seat. The fear that had weighed her down lifted at last.

We made it.

"Yes, but what about the others?" Koenig's voice was heavy with sadness. "All the men who did not make their way here."

"Maybe they did," Susan said. "We don't know yet."

Susan drove up to the trucks. The three of them got out and greeted the British soldiers.

"Has anyone else arrived from Bir Hakeim?" Koenig asked.

The answer was blunt. "No."

The British directed Susan and the others to a Free French position nearby. They also had no word about Bir Hakeim.

"It is my worst fear," Koenig said. "All the men gone. Because of my decisions."

One of the officers tried to comfort him. "Perhaps not, General. We thought you were dead, and here you are."

Koenig shook his head.

While Koenig and Amilakhvari talked to the other French officers, Susan drove the car to the camp's workshop.

"I can't believe this thing is still running," the chief mechanic told her. "There are bullet holes all over. Dozens of them! And you wore out your shock absorbers."

"I'm not surprised," Susan replied, remembering

all the holes she had raced over.

"The brakes are almost gone, too," the mechanic said. "And look at this! A bullet went straight through the seat, right between you and your passengers. It's a miracle you made it!"

"Oh!" Susan stared at the bullet hole. *When did that happen?* she wondered.

It *was* a miracle. Why had they made it when nobody else had? It didn't make sense.

Susan was too exhausted to deal with such a big question. She lay down in the shade of a car, as she had so many times before, and fell into a troubled sleep.

When she woke up, it was late in the afternoon. She stretched, rubbed her bleary eyes—and saw men and vehicles moving slowly toward the camp in the distance.

"It can't be." She looked again, and then a broad smile split her face.

Against all odds, the men and vehicles approaching were the Free French forces from Bir Hakeim!

Chapter 11

MORE WORK STILL TO DO

Cairo, Egypt–Summer 1942

Later that summer, Susan stood on a platform under the blistering Egyptian sun in a military camp just outside of Cairo. She was there to receive the French Croix de Guerre for the role she had played in the escape from Bir Hakeim. Behind her, a military band played the regimental song of the Thirteenth Demi-Brigade of the French Foreign Legion, "Under the Burning Sun of Africa." She couldn't help but think it was appropriate to the occasion.

General Georges Catroux stepped forward and looked out over the crowd. "I am pleased to be here today. It is an honor to present Adjutant Susan Travers with the Croix de Guerre. It is an award given for acts of bravery. The official report says that Miss Travers demonstrated courage and composure as she drove the general's car through a minefield under enemy fire during the sortie from Bir Hakeim. Her bravery in the face of intense artillery fire brought General Koenig and Colonel Amilakhvari to safety." The general looked up from the official citation with a small smile. "Unofficially, several soldiers who were there told me that Miss Travers put her head down and stomped on the gas, totally focused on getting the job done."

Catroux turned to Susan. "Good job, Adjutant Travers." He pinned the medal to her lapel and saluted.

Susan stood at attention and looked out at the audience. It was a small crowd, but everyone who mattered was there: General Koenig, Colonel Amilakhvari, and the men from the Thirteenth Demi-Brigade. Seeing them, she stood a little taller. She was proud of the honor she had received. She was prouder of being their comrade-in-arms.

THE CROIX DE GUERRE AND THE
LEGION OF HONOR

The Croix de Guerre and the Legion of Honor are the highest French military awards.

The Croix de Guerre (Cross of War) was created in World War I. It is awarded to someone who is "mentioned in dispatches." This means that they performed an act of bravery that a superior officer described in an official report. Both individuals and groups can receive the reward. (In a few cases, an entire town has received the medal!)

There are four different levels of Croix de Guerre medals. A small pin attached to the medal's ribbon shows the level of the award: either a bronze star, a silver gilt star or a bronze palm. Susan Travers received a Croix de Guerre with a bronze star. During World War II, both the Vichy government and the Free French forces awarded the Croix de Guerre.

The Legion of Honor is an older award given to both members of the military and to civilians for outstanding service to France. Napoleon Bonaparte created it in 1802. It is the highest honor that anyone can receive in France. There are five different levels of the Legion of Honor: grand cross, grand officer, commander, officer, or chevalier (knight). Susan Travers was named a Chevalier of the Legion of Honor.

The successful breakout from Bir Hakeim was in the past. Medals had been awarded. Wounds had healed. The dead had been mourned. But the war was not over. Germany still occupied large portions of France. The First Free French Brigade and the Thirteenth Demi-Brigade still had work to do.

After Bir Hakeim, the brigade was ordered to join the British army in Egypt, where Susan learned that General Bernard Montgomery, the new commander of the British army in Egypt, had given strict orders that no women were allowed at the front. Female staff members were turned back by military police at every British checkpoint.

As usual, Susan didn't think the rules applied to her. She had survived Bir Hakeim and driven through minefields. She wasn't going to let a bossy British general separate her from her brigade. She was sure she could get through the checkpoints unnoticed. With her hair cropped short, her skin battered by the desert sun, and her mannish khaki uniform, there was nothing feminine about her. The woman who had worn chic Parisian suits and fluttering silk dresses before the war was long gone.

Driving General Koenig's car, Susan passed one checkpoint after another with no trouble. But then one military policeman took a closer look at her. His eyes narrowed in suspicion.

Like the police officers at the earlier checkpoints, he spoke only to the general. "I'm sorry, sir, could I see your driver's papers?"

Koenig roared at the soldier. "I'm a French general on urgent business for General Montgomery. I do not have time for this nonsense!"

The officer waved them through.

Susan was there through the battle at El Alamein. Nobody could stop her.

Susan continued to serve alongside the legion as a driver for the rest of the war: in Italy, in southern France, and in a bitter-cold winter campaign on the border between Germany and France. She usually drove an ambulance, but she did whatever was needed. She even drove a self-propelled anti-tank gun for a short time.

One day, Susan was carrying a wounded legionnaire away from the front when she met a jeep going at full speed in the opposite direction.

The young soldier who was driving it stopped and yelled, "It's over! It's over!"

"What's over?" Susan asked him.

The soldier jumped out of the jeep and ran toward her. "The war, it's over! They've signed an armistice."

For a moment, Susan couldn't believe it. Then she let out a great cheer. *We did it*, she thought. *We won!*

When the celebrations were over, Susan wasn't sure what to do next. For five years, her war work had defined her life. And now it was gone. She had changed too much to fit into the life she'd led before the war. Hunting parties and fancy balls seemed meaningless now. There was nothing for her back in England.

Work was hard to find in Paris. Susan found an administrative job helping the one hundred thousand foreign refugees who flooded into the city at the end of the war. It was important work, but she never felt like she belonged there.

The French Foreign Legion was the only place that felt like home, and she missed it dreadfully.

One day she was talking to an old friend from

the legion, Captain Gabriel Brunet de Sairigné.

"It's a pity you're not a man," he said. "You could join the legion officially."

Susan thought about all the times that she had done something that "women couldn't do."

"Maybe I should," she said.

"It's not possible." He scowled at her across the table. "Women aren't allowed to join the legion."

"I'm not just any woman," she said. "I'm La Miss, Adjutant Travers of Bir Hakeim. I'm halfway in the legion already."

De Sairigné argued with her for the rest of the meal, but Susan wasn't dissuaded.

She made an appointment with another old friend from the Thirteenth Demi-Brigade. Major Paul Arnault was now an official at the legion's recruitment office.

Unlike Captain de Sairigné, Arnault encouraged Susan to apply. "The legion is desperate for volunteers. We lost so many men. You know that."

He paused for a moment while they remembered friends who had died in action.

"People are worn out by the war. These days,

only those with no place to go are willing to join. Prisoners of war. Displaced persons."

"Displaced drivers," Susan joked.

Arnault pushed an application form across his desk. "See here. The application does not ask whether you are a man or a woman. The legion assumes all applicants are men." He chuckled. "Our mistake."

Susan smiled and filled out the form right there with Arnault's help. She gave details of her service at Bir Hakeim, her service record for the rest of the war, and a list of her medals. Arnault attached a glowing review, including the citations for her medals. When they were done, she took a deep breath and signed the application: *Travers, Susan May Gillian, British citizen.*

Now all she had to do was cross her fingers and wait.

On June 28, 1945, Susan Travers became the first and only woman accepted as an official member of the French Foreign Legion.

Her career in the Foreign Legion was brief

and uneventful. She was assigned to the logistics division. As a logistical officer, she ran canteens, private clubs that provided drinks and entertainment for the legion's enlisted men, in Tunisia, Morocco, and French Indochina, at the beginning of what would become the Vietnam War.

In 1996, Susan Travers, now eighty-seven years old, walked slowly to the front of the room where General Hugo Geoffrey waited to present her with France's highest military honor, the Legion of Honor. She was a little shaky on her feet, even with her walking stick, but she stood straight and held her head high. General Geoffrey pinned the medal on the lapel of her brown tweed suit and kissed her on both cheeks.

It was a small ceremony in the reception room of the nursing home where she lived. Unlike the day when she received the Croix de Guerre, there was no brass band. Only a few of the men who had been with her at Bir Hakeim attended—men whom she hadn't seen in decades.

It was sixty years overdue, she thought as she

placed the Legion of Honor with the other medals she had received. There were eleven in all. She read the citations that had accompanied them. One line from the citation for the Ordre de l'Armée caught her eye: "In all circumstances, she was an example of the finest qualities of the legion."

"I certainly tried," she said. *"Nec temere nec timide.* Neither afraid nor timid."

AUTHOR'S NOTE

I've been fascinated for a long time by women who did traditionally male jobs in wartime. Susan Travers's story of her escape from Bir Hakeim was new to me, but the roadblocks she faced because she was a woman were not.

Across the Minefields is based on Travers's own account of these events. I used historical accounts of Bir Hakeim, the French Foreign Legion, and World War II to fill in the military context.

In order to focus on the main events of this story, I simplified the timeline in some places. Most of the dialogue in the book is based directly on conversations Travers described in her memoirs. In a few cases, I created new scenes to illustrate what she saw and felt. All the major events in this book are true.

SELECT BIBLIOGRAPHY

Broche, François. *La Cathédrale des Sables, Bir Hakeim (May 26–June 11, 1942).* Éditions Belin/ Humensis. Paris: 2019.

Collier, Richard. *The War in the Desert.* Alexandria, VA: Time-Life Books, 1977.

Geraghty, Tony. *March or Die: A New History of the French Foreign Legion.* New York and Oxford. Facts on File, 1986.

Koenig, General. *Ce jour-là – 10 juin 1942: Bir Hakeim.* Éditions Robert Laffont. Paris: 1971

Lopez, Jean. editor. *World War II Infographics.* London: Thames & Hudson, 2019.

Lormier, Dominique. *La Bataille de Bir Hakeim: Une Résistance Héroïque.* Paris: Calmann-Lévy, 2009.

McLeave, Hugh. *The Damned Die Hard: The Colorful, True Story of the French Foreign Legion.* New York: Saturday Review Press, 1973.

National World War II Museum. "Forgotten Fights: The Free French at Bir Hacheim." https://www.nationalww2museum.org/war/articles/free-french-bir-hacheim-1942.

Porch, Douglas. *The French Foreign Legion: A Complete History of the Legendary Fighting Force.* New York: HarperCollins, 1991.

Sherman, Jill. *Eyewitness to the Role of Women in World War II.* Mankato, MN: The Child's World, 2016.

Taylor, Eric. *Women Who Went to War, 1938–46.* London: Robert Hale, 1988.

Travers, Susan, with Wendy Holden. *Tomorrow to be Brave. A Memoir of the Only Woman Ever to Serve in the French Foreign Legion.* New York: The Free Press, 2000.

Windrow, Martin. *French Foreign Legion 1914–45.* Oxford: Osprey Publishing, 1999.

World War II Map by Map. New York: DK & The Smithsonian Institution, 1999.